TWO LITTLE PENGUINS CALLED FLAPJACK AND WADDLE

Jacques Duquennoy   Georgie Adams

First published in Great Britain in 1994
Reprinted in 1998, 1999, 2000
by Orion Children's Books
a division of the Orion Publishing Group Ltd
Orion House
5 Upper St Martin's Lane
London WC2H 9EA

Originally published in France by Albin Michel Jeunesse
Text copyright © Orion Children's Books 1994
Illustrations copyright © Albin Michel 1994

A catalogue record for this book
is available from the British Library
Printed in Singapore
ISBN 1 85881 110 4

There was once a little penguin called Flapjack.

Flapjack lived at the South Pole, which was a very cold place to be.

When he was a chick, his mother tucked him under her coat to keep him warm.

Soon Flapjack took his first steps to the sea ...

and jumped in!
He flapped his wings
and flipped his feet ...

and before long, he was swimming perfectly.

In a while, Flapjack grew
a shiny waterproof coat.
It kept him warm and dry
in the icy water.

It was just right for tobogganing, too.

Flapjack had a cousin
called Waddle. He lived
on the other side
of the Pole.

When he was young,
Waddle followed his
mother everywhere.
Until one day ...

they went to the sea.

And Waddle dived in!

It wasn't long before
Waddle had grown a fine
coat to keep out the cold.

He went diving every day
and was very good at it.

One morning
a letter arrived
for Flapjack.

Flapjack took his
best pen and
replied straight away.

Dear Waddle,
Thank you for your kind
invitation. I should like to
stay with you. I've never
been to your side of the ;
Pole before. I'll come
as quickly as I can.
Lots of Love,
Flapjack x
P.S. How far is it?

Flapjack discovered that
Waddle lived a long way away.
It was miles to walk and
much too far to swim.

So Flapjack got to work
and made a boat.

Bravely Flapjack began his voyage across the ocean.

First his engine stopped,   then a friend needed help ...

but Flapjack soon set the poor whale free.

Flapjack was not the only one at sea that day. A huge passenger ship came steaming by.

Flapjack shouted, but no one seemed to notice him.

The surf rocked the little boat and turned it over.

Luckily, Flapjack was a
good sailor and knew
what had to be done.
He pulled the boat
the right way up
in no time.

After that, all was well until ... some sharks arrived.

Flapjack was frightened.
The sharks looked fierce
and hungry.

At that moment, the
friendly whale swam by.
With one flip of her
enormous tail, the sharks
turned and fled.

Flapjack sailed around the edge of the world,

into rough seas and a cold wind.

The wind blew
stronger and the
waves got bigger.

Suddenly Flapjack's
little boat was swept
high into the air ...

and was tossed on to a mountain of ice.

By chance, Flapjack had landed on Waddle's REALLY BIG iceberg.

And Waddle was there to meet him.

There were more penguins
waiting for Flapjack
along the shore.

This looks like
home, thought Flapjack.
How strange!

Waddle showed his
cousin how well he
could dive, as they
plunged into
the sea.

Catching fish and shrimp was easy.

But finding the way home was more difficult.

Flapjack and Waddle were lost under the ice!

Suddenly, the ice cracked open wide!

The friendly whale had come to their rescue.

Flapjack stayed with Waddle
for many days, and the
two little penguins became
very best friends.

But Flapjack knew he had
to return home. His family
would be missing him.
The two friends were sad.
Parting was unthinkable!

So Waddle sailed home with Flapjack ...

and Flapjack sailed back with Waddle ...

The plan was to build
A Great Big Boat, big enough
for them to live on and
carry their families from
one side of the Pole
to the other.

And Flapjack and Waddle are still friends to this day!